MOUNTAIN BIKE HERO

BY JAKE MADDOX

ILLUSTRATED BY SEAN TIFFANY

text by Thomas Kingsley Troupe

Jake Maddox books are published by Stone Arch Books
A Capstone Imprint
151 Good Counsel Drive, P.O. Box 669
Mankato, Minnesota 56002
www.capstonepub.com

*Library of Congress Cataloging-in-Publication Data is available on the
Library of Congress website.*

Library Binding: 978-1-4342-2536-8

Summary: Everyone says that Crooked Hill has a curse. But it's the only
good place to go mountain biking in Flatte County. When Jonah's brother
goes down it during a storm, can Jonah beat the Crooked Hill curse?

Art Director: Kay Fraser
Graphic Designer: Hilary Wacholz
Production Specialist: Michelle Biedscheid

Photo Credits: Sean Tiffany (cover, p. 1)

Printed in the United States of America in Stevens Point, Wisconsin.
092010
005934WZS11

TABLE OF CONTENTS

Chapter 1

FALLING FLAT

Jonah stood up on his mountain bike. He pumped his legs hard, building up speed. The wind blew through his hair as he sped down the dirt road. He liked the fresh air in the country, even if it smelled like manure.

"Hey, wait up!" his younger brother, Shawn, called.

Shawn was riding behind Jonah. He was four years younger and four years slower.

I'm always waiting for him, Jonah thought. He slowed down to let Shawn catch up.

"It's really flat out here," Jonah said as Shawn pedaled toward him. "I guess that must be why they call this place Flatte County."

"It all looks the same," Shawn said, a bit out of breath. He looked around at the endless fields of corn and soybeans. "Just farm after farm."

Jonah liked spending weekends at Grandpa's farm. It was fun to help with chores and visit.

Even so, he was glad Grandpa let them bring their mountain bikes. Out in the country, the best thing to do was spend lots of time outside.

Gravel popped under their bike tires as they rode. A tractor's engine rumbled in the distance. Jonah did a wheelie for a few feet before setting the front wheel back down.

"I'd give anything for some hills," Jonah said. "Anything."

Back home, there were parks with winding paved trails. Some paths led riders down steep slopes and through small woods. Out in Flatte County, Jonah could see for miles, but there was nothing to see. It was completely flat.

"Hey, Jonah," Shawn said, smiling his goofy smile. "Race you back!" He took off, riding as fast as he could.

Jonah shook his head. *Little brothers*, he thought. He waited until Shawn was further down the road, then sped after him.

As he rode, Jonah turned and looked at the trail of dust they left behind. It was fun to ride fast, but he wanted to ride somewhere exciting. He wanted to find a place where there were bumps, curves, and hills.

Jonah wanted to really test out his mountain bike.

Chapter 2

OLD CROOKED HILL

Grandpa was waiting for them on the front porch when Jonah and Shawn rode back. A pitcher of lemonade sat on the small table near his chair.

With a knife, Grandpa was carving pieces off a stick. Hunks of bark lay around his dirty work boots.

"How was the ride?" Grandpa called.

"It was okay, I guess," Jonah said.

He hopped off his bike. He parked it on the kickstand and climbed up to the porch. A moment later, Shawn rolled in behind him.

"Hmmm. That doesn't sound so great," Grandpa said. He set his whittling down and picked up the pitcher.

"There's nowhere really exciting to go," Jonah said, taking off his helmet. He grabbed a glass and let Grandpa pour. Shawn joined them on the porch and held his glass out, too.

Jonah took a sip of the lemonade. It was cold and sour, just the way he liked it. He looked out at the three cows in the field. They stood around, lazily chewing.

"When I was younger . . . ," Grandpa began.

Here we go, Jonah thought. *Another story about the olden days.*

"We used to ride down old Crooked Hill. There was a trail that led down a steep hill. At the bottom was what used to be Snake River," Grandpa said. "It's all dried up now. Wasn't much of a river anyway. More like a creek."

"Sounds cool," Shawn said.

"It was," Grandpa said. "But Crooked Hill came with a curse. Any time my friends and I rode down the hill, we'd wipe out. They called it the Crooked Hill Curse."

"Really?" Jonah asked. He smiled. It sounded like one of Grandpa's old tricks.

"Really," Grandpa said. "We'd come home with cuts and bruises every time we tried."

"Where is this Crooked Hill?" Jonah asked. He looked around at the endless cornfields and flat land.

"It's on the far side of town, behind Jeff's Tractor Repair," Grandpa replied. "The trail is probably overgrown. I don't think anyone has been down there in years."

Jonah drank the rest of his lemonade in one gulp. He set the glass down on the table and put his helmet back on.

"I'm going to check it out," Jonah said, hopping off of the porch. In no time, he was on his mountain bike. He turned toward the dirt road that led away from Grandpa's farm.

"Just be careful," Grandpa said, picking up his whittling again.

"I will," Jonah promised.

"I want to go too!" Shawn called.

"You'll just slow me down!" Jonah shouted over his shoulder. Before Shawn could respond, Jonah rode away. He was off to find Crooked Hill.

He was going to beat that curse.

Chapter 3

DOWNHILL *DISASTER*

Jonah coasted down the main road in town. After a few minutes, he reached Jeff's Tractor Repair. The old building had a CLOSED sign in the front window.

He was excited. There was nothing more fun than exploring wooded trails. Beating the curse would be fun, too.

Jonah was sure he could ride to the bottom of Crooked Hill without crashing. How hard could it be?

He'd ridden down tons of hills in the park at home. No Flatte County hill could be that scary.

Behind the shop was a small forest. Just inside the woods, a small line of dirt weaved through the trees. The trail!

"There it is," he whispered.

Jonah pedaled down the trail. It didn't seem like Flatte County anymore. There were birds chirping in the trees. Squirrels skittered along the ground and raced along branches. Jonah couldn't see any cornfields.

"Okay, Crooked Hill," he said. "Let's see what you've got."

Jonah rode along the trail, keeping his eyes on the tricky turns. He avoided trees and large rocks. Overgrown branches snapped at his jeans.

No problem, Jonah thought. His bike bumped over a dip in the trail. He felt a little disappointed. It was much more fun than riding the country roads. He just wasn't sure it was as exciting as Grandpa had said.

Jonah wondered if he'd found the right trail. So far nothing seemed too dangerous.

Then he rounded a bend.

"The hill," Jonah whispered. The path ahead disappeared down into the woods.

He slowed his bike down and looked around. To his left, it seemed as if the trees and everything dropped off into space. He had found the valley and the start of Crooked Hill.

Jonah smiled. Then he took a deep breath and rode on.

Right away, he saw just how steep the hill was. It seemed to go almost straight down. Twists and turns in the trail lay ahead, but Jonah handled them like a pro. He hit a bump and caught some air. He almost bailed, but then he landed back on the path.

Jonah's bike wheels were spinning like crazy as he rode on. Up ahead, he saw that the trail had a sharp right turn. It followed the slope of the hill. Anyone who missed the turn would drop off the trail and into the valley.

He reached for his brakes, but before Jonah knew it, his tires struck something. He flew up and over the handlebars and landed hard on the trail. His bike slid along the path a few feet and fell over near a tree.

"Ugh," Jonah groaned. He lay there for a moment. He had the wind knocked out of him. His knee hurt like crazy. He was also sure he had scraped his elbow up pretty good.

Once he caught his breath, Jonah sat up and looked back at the trail. There, hidden beneath some low branches, was a tree root. It made a bump in the path.

So that's what I hit, Jonah thought. He stood up, and his knee throbbed in pain. He limped over and picked his bike up. There was dirt all over the pedals, and the front reflector had snapped off. And his bike chain had snapped. He wouldn't be riding his bike for a while.

Great, Jonah thought. *Just great.*

The curse of Crooked Hill was real.

Chapter 4

BUSTED UP

Jonah slowly walked his bike up the trail. His knee hurt, making it hard for him to walk. The long, steep trail didn't help either. It would be suppertime before he reached Grandpa's farm. And then he'd have to tell Grandpa the curse was real.

At the top of the trail, Jonah glanced back. He wondered how far down he'd gone. He couldn't see the dried-up riverbed through all the trees.

I know I can make it to the bottom, Jonah thought. He was just bummed it wouldn't be today.

Jonah found his way to the edge of the woods. He looked at the tractor repair shop, wishing it was open. He could call Grandpa to come pick him up.

He wished Shawn was there, too. Jonah felt bad for leaving him behind at Grandpa's. If Shawn had come, at least he'd have someone to talk to.

But that hill is too dangerous for little kids, Jonah thought. *And not-so-little kids, too, I guess.*

He took his helmet off and hung it over the handlebars. He didn't like wearing it, but he was glad he'd had it on. The last thing he needed was to bang his head up.

Jonah felt strange walking through town with his bike. The broken bike chain dragged on the ground. People looked at him and frowned. He knew it was probably because they didn't know him. Folks in small towns knew each other. That's what Grandpa said, anyway.

A man in an old, beat-up pickup truck pulled up next to Jonah. "Are you all right, son?" the man asked.

Jonah nodded. "I'm fine. Just took a nasty spill," he said.

"Crooked Hill?" the man asked.

"Yeah," Jonah said. "How'd you know?"

"I've wiped out plenty of times on that hill," the man said. "Back when I was a boy, of course. You know, they say there's a curse on that hill."

Jonah smiled. "That's what I've heard," he said.

The man offered Jonah a ride back to his grandpa's.

"I'll walk," Jonah said. "But thanks anyway." He wasn't in any hurry to get back and admit he'd crashed. It was bad enough that he'd messed his bike up.

"Well, be careful, kid," the man replied. "You could really get hurt on that hill."

I know what you mean, Jonah thought as the man drove off.

Chapter 5

MORNING CHORES

"Up and at 'em, boys," Grandpa said as he came into Jonah and Shawn's room the next morning. He opened their curtains so that light streamed into the room. "Breakfast is ready, and we have plenty to do today!"

Jonah groaned and pulled the covers over his head. He was sore from his crash and long walk back. Getting up early to do the farm chores made his muscles ache.

Grandpa hadn't been mad that he crashed his bike, but he said Jonah was going to have to keep doing his responsibilities.

He heard Shawn slide out of his bed and head toward the door.

"Are you still mad at me?" Jonah asked through his pillow.

"Yes," Shawn said. "I wanted to ride down the hill, too."

Jonah sat up, and his knee throbbed. "Be glad you didn't," he told his brother. "You might've ended up like me."

Shawn shrugged. "Whatever," he said. Then he left the room.

Jonah stood up and followed him. He was hungry, and breakfast at Grandpa's was always amazing.

Ever since Jonah could remember, there was always enough food at Grandpa's breakfasts to feed an army.

"Anything you guys don't eat, the dog will," Grandpa said. "Now, who wants pancakes?"

Jonah and Shawn ate until they were full. Then they helped Grandpa clean up and got dressed.

"I'll meet you near the barn, boys," Grandpa called. The screen door banged shut behind him.

"I said I was sorry, Shawn," Jonah said as the boys made their way outside to help Grandpa with the chores. "Are you going to stay mad all day?"

"Maybe," Shawn said. He wouldn't look at Jonah.

They met Grandpa out by the big barn. He was wearing his work overalls and his boots. He whistled as his grandsons came over.

"You boys look tired," Grandpa said. Jonah guessed a big smile was hidden somewhere in his beard. "The quicker we get done, the quicker we can take it easy."

They worked most of the morning. First, they fed the animals. Grandpa let the cows out to pasture, and together they cleaned the pens out. It was gross, smelly work but it had to be done.

Once the pens were clean, Shawn collected eggs from the chicken coop while Jonah and Grandpa milked the cows.

"What should we do now, Grandpa?" Jonah asked when the cows were done being milked.

"Let's get your bike chain fixed," Grandpa said.

They went into the garage. Grandpa flipped Jonah's bike upside down and went to work. He tapped a small piece of metal into the chain, linking them together. In no time, Jonah's bike was fixed.

"Almost like new," Grandpa said. He lifted the bike up and set it on its tires.

"Awesome," Jonah said. "I want to give Crooked Hill another try."

Grandpa shook his head. "Not today, Crash," he said.

He led Jonah out of the garage and pointed to the sky. Dark clouds gathered over to the west. The sky flashed, and there was a faraway rumble. A thunderstorm was coming.

"Oh, great," Jonah said. It didn't look like he'd be riding any time soon.

"Find Shawn, and we'll get the animals inside," Grandpa said.

Jonah headed around the side of the barn to the chicken coop. Shawn wasn't in there. As Grandpa brought the pigs to their little metal huts, Jonah ran inside the farmhouse.

"Shawn?" Jonah called, but there was no answer. In the kitchen, he saw a basket of eggs. Shawn had finished his chore.

Jonah went back outside and looked everywhere. There was no sign of Shawn.

"Oh no," Jonah whispered.

Shawn's mountain bike was missing, too.

Chapter 6

SHAWN'S GONE!

"Grandpa!" Jonah yelled.

Jonah ran across the yard. Grandpa was leading the cows to the barn. In the distance, the storm grew louder.

"What's going on?" Grandpa asked. He latched the barn door and wiped his hands on his overalls. "Where's Shawn?"

"I don't know," Jonah said. "He's not here. His bike is gone and everything."

Together, Grandpa and Jonah ran along the edges of the fields. They called Shawn's name and looked for bike tracks in the grass.

"We've got to find him," Grandpa said. "Come on. We'll have to take my truck."

"He could've gone into town," Jonah said as they hurried toward the driveway. "Maybe he went to buy some baseball cards."

"It's worth a try," Grandpa said. "Hop in the truck."

"Just a second," Jonah said. "I need something." He raced over to the barn. He pulled his mountain bike over to the truck. His helmet was slung over the handlebars. With a grunt, he lifted his bike into the back of the pickup.

"Why are you bringing your bike?" Grandpa asked as Jonah hopped into the truck.

"I can ride around town and look for him," Jonah said. "We'll cover more ground that way."

"If the storm gets worse, you'll have to wait in a store," Grandpa said. "It could be dangerous. You'll have to be very careful."

"I know," Jonah said. "But we have to find Shawn."

* * *

Giant raindrops fell as they pulled into town. The storm was getting closer, and people were running to their cars. When Grandpa slowed to a stop, Jonah hopped out. He pulled his bike out of the back and strapped his helmet on.

"I'll head up the main street," Grandpa said. "Can you ride behind some of the shops to look for him?"

"Sure," Jonah said. He looked up at the sky. The storm could get much worse.

Grandpa drove off as Jonah rode through the wet streets, calling for his brother.

People stood inside the stores, waiting for the rain to stop. Jonah's wet T-shirt stuck to his skin.

He turned off the street and tore through a small gap between the grocery store and the diner. The backs of the stores were cluttered with old boxes, wooden pallets, and garbage dumpsters. There was no sign of Shawn.

In the distance, thunder boomed.

Jonah did a hard turn and skidded around the corner. "Shawn!" he called.

Nothing.

Jonah returned to the main street. Grandpa's truck was in the middle of the road. He was talking to a guy in a baseball cap and overalls.

"Jonah, come over here!" Grandpa yelled from the truck's window.

With rain in his eyes, Jonah raced to the pickup.

"Bill says he saw a kid riding that way," Grandpa said. He pointed down the road.

Jonah turned and looked through the rain. Down at that end of town were a few empty buildings and Jeff's Tractor Repair.

"Of course," Jonah shouted. "I know where Shawn went!"

Chapter 7

RACING THE RAIN

"Do you really think he'd go to Crooked Hill alone?" Grandpa asked. He helped Jonah lift his bike into the back of the pickup. "Even after your big wipeout?"

"That's exactly why he went," Jonah replied. "He wants to try to beat the curse!"

They got into the truck. Grandpa turned the windshield wipers as fast as they would go. They swished back and forth across the window.

It didn't do much good. The rain was really coming down.

"I should have let him come with me," Jonah said.

"This isn't your fault," Grandpa said. He drove toward Jeff's Tractor Repair shop. He squinted through the windshield. The sky was dark with storm clouds.

"Maybe Shawn already headed back to the farm," Grandpa said. "We might get lucky."

Jonah hoped so. He wasn't sure how he'd find his brother if he was down the Crooked Hill trail. With the darkness and rain, it wouldn't be easy.

They climbed out of the truck and looked around. Jonah cupped his hands around his mouth. "Shawn!" he yelled.

"I'm not sure he'll be able to hear you," Grandpa said. "Not with the thunder and rain coming down like this."

Jonah sighed. He knew what he had to do.

"Can you help me get my bike out, Grandpa?" Jonah asked. He tightened the strap on his helmet.

Grandpa's eyes were wide. "You can't ride down there, Jonah! Not in this weather!" he said.

"I don't have a choice," Jonah replied. "If Shawn's down there, that's the only way I'll find him. Walking will take too long. The lightning is getting closer."

Grandpa scratched his head. He nodded finally. Then he helped Jonah lift his mountain bike from the back of the pickup.

"How's your knee?" Grandpa asked. He set the bike onto the ground. "Is it still sore?"

"I'm fine," Jonah said. He added, "I heal quickly."

"I should go with you," Grandpa said. "It's too dangerous."

"Someone has to stay behind in case Shawn shows up," Jonah said.

"Good point. Just be careful, buddy," Grandpa warned. "I don't like this idea."

"I don't either," Jonah replied.

Before Grandpa could change his mind, Jonah hopped on his bike. He pedaled to the edge of the woods.

The woods seemed different. They reminded Jonah of a rainforest.

Water poured through the leaves and ran down the trees. The trail was muddy and dotted with puddles.

Jonah's bike tires splashed through the trail. He felt mud splatter up his back.

The beginning of the hill was up ahead. Jonah squeezed the brakes and heard them squeak. Wet brakes were never good.

"Shawn! Can you hear me?" Jonah's yell was lost in the storm. He tried to listen past the patter of raindrops and the rumbling sky. Somewhere, off in the distance, he heard something.

A voice!

"Help! I'm down here!" Shawn yelled.

Jonah's heart beat fast. His little brother was down Crooked Hill!

Chapter 8

MUDDY RIDE

"I'm coming, Shawn!" Jonah yelled.

Jonah took a deep breath and pedaled down the muddy trail. Waves of water ran down the path like a river.

His wheels slipped along, and Jonah was afraid he would crash before he found his brother.

The mountain bike picked up speed. Mud coated the bike and the legs of his jeans.

To his left, he saw a flash of lightning. It was on the other side of the valley. The storm was getting closer.

"Hurry, Jonah!" Shawn's voice sounded small and far away.

Raindrops made it hard for Jonah to see. *This is crazy,* Jonah thought. *I'm going to wipe out any second. Then we'll both be stuck out here.*

With his fingers ready to squeeze the brakes, Jonah and his mountain bike tore down the trail. Puddles sprayed up at him as his tires blasted through them.

Even though it was hard to see, Jonah knew the nasty tree root — the one that had tripped up his bike the day before — was close. He squinted to see it, but his eyes were blurry from the rain.

He pulled gently on his brakes, but they didn't slow him down. The wet wheels just squeaked and the bike picked up even more speed.

The back tire slid sideways. Jonah was sure he'd crash. He quickly steered to the right and caught his balance. A loud clap of thunder made his bones rattle and the ground shake.

Where is Shawn? Jonah wondered.

Suddenly, he felt a jolt as his bike slammed into the root.

This time, Jonah held on tight. He felt the wheels leap off of the muddy trail. The bike was in the air for a second and then landed on both tires.

"Nice!" Jonah shouted. His heart was pumping fast but he kept going.

"Where are you, Shawn?" Jonah shouted.

He turned a corner. Now he was racing down a part of the trail he'd never seen.

"Here! I see you! I'm down a little further!" Shawn yelled. His voice was closer.

Even though he was already going fast, Jonah pumped the pedals. He knew he had to beat the lightning.

Jonah's tires ripped through the mud, and his bike bunny-hopped over the bigger rocks. Wet branches smacked his helmet as he flew past. Jonah avoided a fallen tree in the path and almost went over the edge.

"I'm here!" Shawn called from up ahead. His bike was in a heap on the trail. He sat against an old, rotten tree, rubbing his arm.

Jonah tried to brake, but it was no use. His brakes were too wet.

He put his legs down and dug his feet into the trail. His shoes were coated with mud, but he was able to stop.

He set his bike down and ran to his brother. "What happened? Are you okay?" Jonah asked. Shawn shivered and nodded. Then he pointed to his bike.

"It's ruined," Shawn cried. "I wrecked it!"

Jonah looked over. The front wheel of Shawn's mountain bike was bent. He'd hit something hard.

"Can you walk?" Jonah asked.

"I don't think so," Shawn said. "I twisted my right ankle trying to stop. Then I fell on my arm."

Jonah pulled the pant leg of Shawn's jeans up a little.

"Careful," Shawn warned. "It hurts."

Shawn's right ankle looked bad. It was swollen, puffy, and definitely twisted.

Thunder boomed above them.

"Okay," Jonah said. "Let's get you out of here."

Chapter 9

UPHILL BATTLE

Jonah helped Shawn onto his left foot. Shawn slipped in the mud and cried out. Lightning struck closer to them, down in the river valley.

"Sorry," Jonah said. Then he crouched down. "Climb onto my back."

Shawn said, "What about the bikes?"

"Can't ride them in this storm," Jonah replied. "It's too dangerous. We'll get them tomorrow."

Shawn climbed onto his brother's back. Their clothes were muddy and slippery, but he held on.

"Ready?" Jonah asked. He felt the ache in his knee return.

"I guess so," Shawn said, holding on.

Jonah looked at their bikes. He hoped they wouldn't get washed away into the valley. But he knew he couldn't carry Shawn and the bikes.

With a deep breath, Jonah headed slowly back up the hill. He was careful not to shift Shawn around too much.

"Is Grandpa mad at me?" Shawn asked.

"I don't think so," Jonah said. "He was just really worried. We didn't know where you went. I should've guessed you'd be here."

"I just wanted to try the hill," Shawn said quietly. "I wanted to show you I could do it."

Jonah smiled. "You made it down the hill further than I did," he said. "Guess you're a better biker than I am."

Shawn laughed, but stopped suddenly. "Oh, that hurts," he groaned.

The muscles in Jonah's legs ached. Even though Shawn was small, he was still heavy. It didn't matter. Jonah knew they had to reach the top of the hill and find Grandpa's truck.

Thunder rumbled again. Shawn held on tighter. Water rushed down the mud path, soaking Jonah's shoes. The ground was slippery. More than a few times, he thought he was going to fall.

"The storm is getting worse," Shawn said. "How much farther?"

Jonah looked. Up ahead he spotted the wicked tree root in the path. They were making progress, even if it was slow.

"We're almost there," he said.

Just then, a bolt of lightning struck a tree about forty feet in front of them. The flash of light was blinding. Jonah was sure his heart was going to stop. With a crack, the tree began to fall. It teetered toward them!

"Hang on!" Jonah shouted and dashed off of the trail, carrying Shawn. A second later, the tree came down. It crashed down onto the path and the ground shook. The tree was nearly split down the middle. Jonah could smell burnt wood.

"That was way too close," Shawn cried. "This hill really is cursed!"

No one back home will believe this, Jonah thought. *My friends will think I'm making stuff up.*

Once he caught his breath, Jonah ran as fast as he could. He darted between the trees and through giant mud puddles. Jonah kept his eyes on the trail. He didn't want to get lost in the woods.

Finally, they reached the top of the hill.

"There!" Shawn shouted. "I see Grandpa's truck!"

Chapter 10

BREAKING THE CURSE

Jonah pushed through the trees to the clearing behind Jeff's Tractor Repair.

"Boys!" Grandpa called. He ran over to them, his clothes soaked. He lifted Shawn off of Jonah's back. Jonah dropped to the ground, exhausted.

"I saw the lightning and heard the tree fall," Grandpa said. "I was worried sick. I almost called the police to have them look for you."

"We're fine, Grandpa," Jonah said and rolled onto his back. Cool rain dropped onto his face. "Shawn twisted his ankle."

"I'll live," Shawn said. "I'm just glad to be out of there!"

Jonah sat up. He glanced at the woods one last time, then got to his feet.

"You almost got us, Crooked Hill," Jonah whispered. "Almost."

"Let's go, Jonah!" Grandpa yelled.

The three of them spent the next few hours in the doctor's office. Shawn had his ankle wrapped up and iced. The doctor said it would be fine in a few days.

Once the storm cleared, the sun came back out. It warmed up the fields, making mist rise. To Jonah, it looked like a scene from a horror movie.

They ate a late lunch at the diner. All of the other customers were talking about the storm.

Other trees in Flatte County had been struck by lightning. Luckily, no one knew of any damage to buildings, and everyone was safe.

"Your mom and dad will be here soon," Grandpa said. "We should probably go get your bikes."

Jonah nodded. "I sure don't want to walk back down Crooked Hill," he said. "But we can't just leave our mountain bikes down there."

After they paid for their meal, they climbed into Grandpa's pickup. He headed back toward the south end of town. He parked behind Jeff's Tractor Repair.

All of them got out, Shawn carefully limping next to Jonah. They gazed into the woods.

"I bet there's a river down there, now," Jonah said. "It rained enough to fill it back up."

"It sure did," Grandpa said. "But it won't last. Snake River's been dry since I was a boy."

Jonah gazed into the woods. "Grandpa, when I get back up with the bikes," he said. "Do you think I could try the hill one more time?"

Grandpa put a hand on Jonah's shoulder. "Why would you ever want to do that?" Grandpa asked.

Jonah nodded toward the woods. "You know," he said. "To try to break the curse."

"I'd say you already did, Jonah," Grandpa said. "You rode it in the worst storm we've seen in years. You didn't wipe out on your way to find Shawn. A tree falling on the path didn't even stop you."

Grandpa ruffled his hair. "You beat the curse, kid," Grandpa said. "Hands down."

Jonah smiled and nodded. "Yeah," he said. "I guess I did." He looked at Shawn. "I'm sorry again that I left you behind," he said.

"And I'm sorry I left without telling you guys where I was going," Shawn said.

Grandpa laughed. "Yeah?" he said. "Well, I'm sorry I ever told you boys about this dumb hill."

All three of them laughed as they gazed into the woods.

MORE ABOUT

Mountain biking is an awesome way to have fun. There are tons of cool tricks and stunts, and it can be really exciting. However, it's really important to follow safety guidelines whenever you're on a bike. Here are just a few of them.

- Always wear a helmet, even if you're just going a short distance. Helmets protect your skull and brain!

- Know the road or trail you're riding on. If you can, travel it by foot first. That way you can spot hidden obstacles or problem spots.

- Remember — the pros you see on TV have been mountain biking for years. They have training and real-life experience. Don't expect to have skills like a pro when you first start out.

MOUNTAIN BIKING

- Make sure someone knows where you are when you're out biking. If you can, bring a buddy.

- Get trained. Many cities have mountain-biking classes. Sign up with a friend so you'll have someone to ride with.

- Keep your bike in good shape. Check the tires each time you ride. If the frame gets damaged, fix it right away.

- If you fall — which you probably will — don't let it get you down! Everyone falls. If you've protected yourself by wearing a helmet, and you've learned how to ride, you'll be okay. Just get back on and keep going!

HAPPY RIDING

ABOUT THE AUTHOR

Thomas Kingsley Troupe is a freelance writer, filmmaker, and firefighter/EMT. He is the author of many books for kids of all ages, and he's worked on the visual effects crews of numerous feature movies. His love of action and adventure is often reflected in his stories and films. Thomas lives in Minnesota with his wife and young sons.

ABOUT THE ILLUSTRATOR

When Sean Tiffany was growing up, he lived on a small island off the coast of Maine. Every day until he graduated from high school, he had to take a boat to get to school! Sean has a pet cactus named Jim.

GLOSSARY

COMPLETELY (kuhm-PLEET-lee)—totally, in every way

CREEK (KREEK)—a small stream, smaller than a river

CURSE (KURSS)—bad luck that is said to exist in a place

FIELD (FEELD)—a piece of open land, used for growing crops or playing sports

KICKSTAND (KIK-stand)—on a bicycle, a piece of metal or plastic that keeps the bike in an upright position while it's stopped

MANURE (muh-NOO-ur)—animal waste put on land to improve the quality of the soil and help crops grow better

OVERGROWN (oh-vur-GROHN)—not taken care of; grown too much

PASTURE (PASS-chur)—grazing land for animals

RESPONSIBILITIES (ri-spon-suh-BIL-uh-teez)—jobs or duties

WHITTLING (WIT-uhl-ing)—something someone makes out of wood by cutting it with a small knife

DISCUSSION QUESTIONS

1. Why did Shawn want to ride down Crooked Hill, even though he knew Jonah had hurt himself?

2. Jonah loves mountain biking. What's your favorite thing to do outside? Why?

3. Do you have a sibling? How do you feel about him or her? Talk about it.

WRITING PROMPTS

1. Pretend you're Jonah. Write a letter to your best friend, describing what happened while you were at Grandpa's house.

2. There are many illustrations in this book. Which one is your favorite? Choose one, and draw your own version.

3. What do you think happens after this story ends? Write a chapter that tells what happens next.

EXPLORE

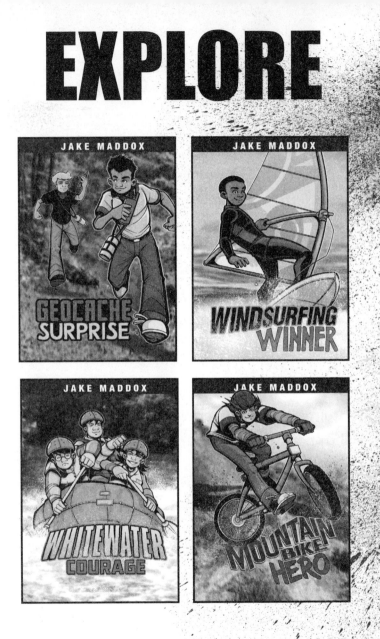